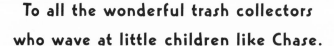

To all the wonderful trash collectors
who wave at little children like Chase.
—A.Z. & D.C.

To litterbugs everywhere.
—D.Y.

Trashy Town
Text copyright © 1999 by Andrea Zimmerman and David J. Clemesha
Illustrations copyright © 1999 by Dan Yaccarino
Printed in the U.S.A. All rights reserved.
Visit our web site at http://www.harperchildrens.com.

Library of Congress Cataloging-in-Publication Data
Zimmerman, Andrea Griffing.
Trashy Town / by Andrea Zimmerman & David Clemesha; pictures by Dan Yaccarino.
p. cm.   Summary: Little by little, can by can, Mr. Gilly, the trash man, cleans up his town.
ISBN 0-06-027139-6. — ISBN 0-06-027140-X (lib. bdg.)   [1. Refuse and refuse
disposal—Fiction.] I. Clemesha, David. II. Yaccarino, Dan, ill. III. Title.
PZ7.Z618Tr 1999   98-27495
[E]—dc21   CIP
                                                                          AC

1 2 3 4 5 6 7 8 9 10
❖
First Edition

TRASHY TOWN

Andrea Zimmerman and David Clemesha
illustrated by Dan Yaccarino

HarperCollins*Publishers*

Mr. Gilly is a trashman.

In the morning, Mr. Gilly puts on
his heavy gloves. He climbs into his
big trash truck.

He turns the key. He drives his empty truck down the street. He is looking for trash.

STOP!

There are trash cans by the school.

Mr. Gilly empties the cans into the truck.

Dump it in, smash it down, drive around the Trashy Town!

Is the trash truck full yet?

NO.

Mr. Gilly drives on.

STOP!

There are trash cans in the park.

Mr. Gilly empties the cans into the truck.

Dump it in, smash it down, drive around the Trashy Town!

Is the trash truck full yet?

NO.

Mr. Gilly drives on.

STOP!

There are
trash cans
behind
the pizza
parlor.

Mr. Gilly
empties
the cans
into the
truck.

Dump it in, smash it down, drive around the Trashy Town!

Is the trash truck full yet?

NO.

Mr. Gilly drives on.

*S*TOP!

There are trash cans next to the doctor's office.

Mr. Gilly empties the cans into the truck.

Dump it in, smash it down, drive around the Trashy Town!

Is the trash truck full yet?

NO.

Mr. Gilly drives on.

STOP!

There are trash cans by the fire station.

Mr. Gilly empties the cans into the truck.

Dump it in, smash it down, drive around the Trashy Town!

Is the trash truck full yet?

NO.

Mr. Gilly drives down all the streets in Trashy Town.

He empties all the trash cans into the truck.

Dump it in, smash it down, drive around the Trashy Town!

Is the trash truck full yet?

YES!

Mr. Gilly has cleaned up
the whole town!

Mr. Gilly drives the full trash truck to the dump.

Up, up, up goes the truck. Down, down, down goes the trash.

I dumped
it in.
I smashed
it down.

I love
to
clean
up
Trashy
Town!

Mr. Gilly turns off the key.
He takes off his gloves.
Then he goes home.